Dear Parents:

Congratulations! Your child is taking the first steps on an exciting journey. The destination? Independent reading!

STEP INTO READING® will help your child get there. The program offers five steps to reading success. Each step includes fun stories and colorful art or photographs. In addition to original fiction and books with favorite characters, there are Step into Reading Non-Fiction Readers, Phonics Readers and Boxed Sets, Sticker Readers, and Comic Readers—a complete literacy program with something to interest every child.

Learning to Read, Step by Step!

Ready to Read   Preschool–Kindergarten
• big type and easy words • rhyme and rhythm • picture clues
For children who know the alphabet and are eager to begin reading.

Reading with Help   Preschool–Grade 1
• basic vocabulary • short sentences • simple stories
For children who recognize familiar words and sound out new words with help.

Reading on Your Own   Grades 1–3
• engaging characters • easy-to-follow plots • popular topics
For children who are ready to read on their own.

Reading Paragraphs   Grades 2–3
• challenging vocabulary • short paragraphs • exciting stories
For newly independent readers who read simple sentences with confidence.

Ready for Chapters   Grades 2–4
• chapters • longer paragraphs • full-color art
For children who want to take the plunge into chapter books but still like colorful pictures.

STEP INTO READING® is designed to give every child a successful reading experience. The grade levels are only guides; children will progress through the steps at their own speed, developing confidence in their reading.

Remember, a lifetime love of reading starts with a single step!

Copyright © 2021 Disney Enterprises, Inc. All rights reserved. Published in the United States by Random House Children's Books, a division of Penguin Random House LLC, 1745 Broadway, New York, NY 10019, and in Canada by Penguin Random House Canada Limited, Toronto, in conjunction with Disney Enterprises, Inc.

Step Into Reading, Random House, and the Random House colophon are registered trademarks of Penguin Random House LLC.

Visit us on the Web!
StepIntoReading.com
rhcbooks.com

Educators and librarians, for a variety of teaching tools, visit us at RHTeachersLibrarians.com

ISBN 978-0-7364-4103-2 (trade) — ISBN 978-0-7364-8295-0 (lib. bdg.)
ISBN 978-0-7364-4104-9 (ebook)

Printed in the United States of America   10 9 8 7 6 5 4 3

DISNEY

Raya
AND
THE LAST DRAGON

THE FIGHT FOR KUMANDRA

adapted by Natasha Bouchard

illustrated by the Disney Storybook Art Team

Random House 🏠 New York

The Land of Heart is beautiful.

It holds the magical Dragon Gem.

A fierce warrior protects
the Dragon Gem.
His name is Chief Benja.
A determined girl named Raya
tries to get past him.
She dodges, rolls, and leaps!

Raya reaches the Gem!

Chief Benja is her father.

He is proud of his daughter.

Raya is now a Guardian

of the Dragon Gem.

Chief Benja invites people from
Tail, Spine, Talon, and Fang
to the Land of Heart.

He wants to unite

the five lands of Kumandra.

But they do not trust one another.

Raya meets Namaari, who is
from the Land of Fang.
Both girls love dragons.
Raya trusts her new friend,
so she brings Namaari
to the Dragon Gem.

Namaari tricks **Raya**.

She tries to steal the Gem!

Hearing the noise,

more guests arrive.

They all want the Dragon Gem.

Chief Benja protects it.

Chief Benja is hurt.

Everyone tries to grab the Gem,

and it breaks into five pieces!

Then the Druun appear.

They can turn people to stone.

Chief Benja gives Raya

a Gem piece to protect her

from the Druun.

He throws her into the river.

The Druun turn

Chief Benja to stone.

Six years later,

Raya and her friend Tuk Tuk

look for the last dragon.

The dragon's magic

can bring Raya's father back.

Raya finds the end of a river.

She hopes the dragon is here.

She offers food and asks

for the dragon's help.

Suddenly, the dragon appears!

Her name is Sisu.

Raya asks Sisu to make a new Gem.

But it is impossible.

They will need to find

all the Dragon Gem pieces.

They find a Gem piece
in the Land of Tail.
Its magic transforms
Sisu into a human.

With no warning, Namaari shows up.

She has been tracking Raya.

Raya and Sisu escape

by jumping onto a shrimp boat.

Raya and Sisu meet Boun.

He is the captain

of the shrimp boat.

He agrees to take them to Talon

to look for the next Gem piece.

The group arrives in Talon.

Raya warns Sisu

not to trust anyone.

But Sisu wanders off

with an old woman.

The old woman wants
all the Dragon Gem pieces.
She leads Sisu to a trap!
Raya and Tuk Tuk save Sisu
and take the woman's Gem piece.

A toddler named Noi

and three Ongis join the group.

They are clever and sneaky.

They make a good team.

When the group arrives in Spine,
they meet a warrior named Tong.
They do not trust him at first,
but Tong agrees to help them.
He has a Dragon Gem piece.

The last missing Gem piece is
in the palace of Fang.
Sisu says they should
trust Namaari to help them.
They meet Namaari near Fang.
She brings the final Gem piece.

Namaari threatens Sisu.

Sisu remains calm,

but Raya does not trust Namaari.

Raya pulls out her sword.

The crossbow fires.

An arrow strikes Sisu!

Sisu falls into a canal,

and all the water dries up.

Now Fang is not protected by water.

The Drunn attack Fang

while Raya chases Namaari.

Raya fights Namaari
in Fang Palace.
Raya is angry, but she realizes
that fighting is not the way
to save Kumandra.

Raya finds her team.

If they want to defeat the Druun,

they need to trust each other.

Raya believes in Namaari, too.

She gives Namaari her Gem piece.

She turns to stone.

The team follows Raya.

Namaari trusts Raya's plan.

She puts all the pieces

of the Dragon Gem together.

Then she turns to stone.

At first, nothing happens.

Then a light shines over the land.

The Druun disappear,
and rain falls from the sky.
Sisu and all the dragons return!

All the stone people
come back to life.
Raya hugs her father.
They have finally brought
peace to Kumandra.

BE BRAVE

LET'S ROLL

RAYA

RAYA

© Disney